George Robert Sims

Ballads of Babylon

George Robert Sims

Ballads of Babylon

ISBN/EAN: 9783742899620

Manufactured in Europe, USA, Canada, Australia, Japa

Cover: Foto ©Andreas Hilbeck / pixelio.de

Manufactured and distributed by brebook publishing software
(www.brebook.com)

George Robert Sims

Ballads of Babylon

BALLADS OF
BABYLON.

BY

GEORGE R. SIMS.

AUTHOR OF "THE DAGONET BALLADS."

LONDON:

JOHN P. FULLER,

WINE OFFICE COURT, E.C.

1880.

To JOHN RYDER, ESQ.,

The eminent Actor and Professor of Elocution, these Ballads are dedicated by his sincere Friend and Admirer,

GEORGE R. SIMS.

.

CONTENTS.

MISCELLANEOUS.

BALLADS OF BABYLON.

OVERTURE.

FROM Babylon the mighty, for ever and for
    aye,
    Float the voices of her toilers and the
    fighters in the fray—
Float the voices of her victims high above the
    battle's din,
As they chant in fitful measure all the ballads of her
    sin.

From Babylon the mighty the monster chorus
    swells,
A cry to one vague heaven from all the million
    hells ;
The wail of souls despairing, the curse of maddened
    woe;
The shriek of hunted wretches who flee the ruth-
    less foe.

I hear the half-hushed whisper, the growing mur-
    murs, then
The deep hoarse cry for vengeance of fierce and
    frenzied men—
The wild barbaric music that crashes through the
    spheres,
To die away in echoes of the women's sobs and
    tears.

I hear the lonely singer who wanders from the
    crowd,
Whose song is sung in secret, with blanched face
    earthward bowed,
Who shuns the swollen chorus and seeks His ear
    alone,
To tell a God of sorrows what sorrows men have
    known.

From Babylon the mighty, for ever and for
    aye,
Float the voices of her toilers and the fighters in the
    fray—
Float the voices of her victims high above the
    battle's din,
As they chant in fitful measure all the ballads of her
    sin.

FALLEN BY THE WAY.

ON'T be a fool and blub, Jim, it's a
darned good thing for you—
You'll find a mate as can carry and 'll
play the music too;
I'm done this time, for a dollar—I can hardly get
my breath;
There's something as tells me, somehow, " Bill Joy,
you be took for death."
It's a wessel gone bust, and a big 'un; I can hardly
speak for blood;
It's the last day's tramp as 'as done it—the hills
and the miles o' mud.
There ain't not the sign of a light, Jim, in this
God-forsaken spot—
Hunt for some warter, pardner, for my lips is
burnin' hot.

How much ha' we took to-day, Jim? Why not a
single brown,
And our show was one o' the best once, and we
rode from town to town;
Now it's dirty and old and battered, and the
puppets is wus for wear,
And their arms and their legs is shaky, and their
backs is reg'lar bare.
I ain't done my share o' the work, mate, since I
went that queer in the chest,
But I done what I could, old fellow, and you know
as I did my best;
And now—well, I'm done, I reckon; it's life as is
flowing fast—
Stick to me, Jim—don't leave me; it's the end as
is come at last.

There's Toby a-waggin' his tail there; poor chap,
how he'll miss me, Jim!—
Whoever you takes for mate, mind, they ain't to be
'ard on 'im;
For I 'ad him a six weeks' puppy, and I taught him
to box with Punch—
What was that sound in the distance? I fancied I
heard a scrunch.

Nothin'—ah well, no matter! I thought 'twas a
    footstep p'r'aps.
A traveller as might ha' helped us, or one o' them
    farmer chaps.
A doctor might stop the bleedin'; but there's never
    a chance o' one.
I'll be cold and dead in the mornin'—yer poor old
    pardner's done.

I feel just as if I was chokin' and I'm, O, so faint
    and low;
Prop me agen the boxes, so I can see the
    show—
The dear old show and the puppets, Judy and
    Punch and all;
I'd like just to see 'em again, Jim—so prop me afore
    I fall.
O the miles that we've been together, I and the
    puppets and you
And Toby, our faithful Toby—ah, when the show
    was new!
Do ye think of the time, old fellow, when first we
    took the road,
And *she* was with us, God bless her! and never a
    grief we knowed?

It may be as God'll let her look down from the sky
    to-night,
From out o' the stars up yonder, where she sits in
    the Halls o' Light—
Look down on the poor old showman and see as his
    time is nigh,
And he's comin' to join his darlin' where there's
    never no more Good-bye!
O, Jim, how I well remember the night as my
    sweetheart died,
When she lay by the wee dead baby, only a nine
    months' bride.
'Twas the fall from the stilts as did it, and the wild,
    rough life we led:
D'ye mind what she whispered dyin'—the beautiful
    words she said?

'Twas when she knew she was goin'; I'm seeing
    her wan white cheek
And the sweet sad smile that lit it when she tried so
    hard to speak;
When she took our hands and joined 'em, and bade
    us, through bad and good,
Be pals, and stick tight to each other! and both
    on us said we would.

I knew as you loved her fust, Jim, and had loved
    her all along,
And I see how you 'id yer feelin's when you see as
    you'd counted wrong ;
But you stuck like a pal to the show, Jim, and you
    worked and whistled away,
And *she* never guessed your secret, or she wouldn't
    ha' been so gay.

I fancy the dear old days, Jim, when she was alive,
    poor lass—
The feasts that we had by the hedges, and the chats
    in the long green grass,
And the cosy nights at the taverns, when the coin
    came rolling in :
How we laughed when she puffed our baccy, and
    pretended to drink our gin !
Then Toby, a gay young fellow, would lie by the
    fire and doze,
While the missis worked at the puppets, and altered
    and turned their clo's ;
And Judy and Punch and Joey were never so smart
    before,
And the Ghost had a nice white gown on, as a
    clergyman might ha' wore.

She went in the cruel winter, when the bread was
    hard to get,
When we tramped and slept in the cowsheds, hungry
    and cold and wet.
How far am I from her grave, Jim? Ah, a hundred
    miles maybe;
To lie by the side o' one's darlin' ain't meant for
    the likes o' me.
The parish 'll bury me here, Jim—here where I
    chance to die;
Come to the grave and see me, and bid me a last
    good-bye.
You can bring the show and the puppets, and Toby,
    and beat the drum;
Who knows but that I may hear it in the wonderful
    Kingdom Come?

I'm goin', old pal—don't blubber and look with that
    skeered white face;
Stand by me here to the last, lad; it's a horrible
    lonely place;
Stoop, for I'll have to whisper—O, my eyes grow
    strange and dim,
And I feel like poor old Punch feels when the hang-
    man comes to him.

I warn't much use as a pardner, and I ain't not
    been for a year,
This bustin' o' wessels and corfin' has made me that
    awful queer,
I'd like to ha' got to a willage or ha' crawled as fur
    as a shed:
Jim, if I lose my senses, stay till yer know I'm
    dead.

O, it's hard to die in the open—here on a country
    road ;
That's a matter o' sentymunt, ain't it ? well
    sentymunt jes' be blowed !
For where can a cove die better than under a starlit
    sky,
With his pardner's arms about him, and a tear in
    his pardner's eye ?
Now I want yer to do me a favour—it's the last as
    I'll ask ye, Jim –
There's a mist comin' over my eyeballs, and my
    senses seems to swim ;
Set up the show in the road there—there where the
    moonlight be
Let down the baize and work it, now, while I've
    strength to see.

Give me the drum a minit—I can hardly raise the
    stick ;
Now, are ye ready, pardner ?—up with the curtain,
    quick !
The blood comes faster and faster—that's it!   Ah,
    Punch, old boy,
And Judy, and there's the Baby, and Toby, the
    children's joy.
Poor Toby, he knows there's trouble ; for see how
    he hangs his tail ;
Bark at the Bobby, Toby, he's a-takin' old Punch
    to gaol.
Where have you gone to, pardner ?   Where have
    you put the show ?
I see but the big, black shadows that darker and
    darker grow.

I know what it is—the signal!   Put down the
    pipes and drum.
I'm off to the distant country—the touch on the
    shoulder's come.
Shall I take any message for you, Jim ?   I shall see
    her up there, maybe,
And I'll tell her how hard you worked, mate, and
    the pal as you've been to me.

Jim, when I'm gone I wants yer just to look in the
    box and take
The ragged old dress we kept there and treasured
    for her sweet sake—
The dress that she made for Judy—and lay it upon
    my breast ;
And I want you, the day I'm buried, to give the
    show a rest.

Bring 'em away to the churchyard, and show 'em
    their master's grave.
Now take up your pipes and blow 'em, and tip us a
    farewell stave.
Mind, when you're choosin' a mate, Jim, don't
    have a rogue or muff ;
Make him handle the puppets gentle, for they've
    never been treated rough.
Give me the dog a minit—see how he licks my
    cheek.
Now for a tune on the pipes, mate, and speak as
    the puppets speak ;
It's the music I've lived my life to—let me hear it
    again and die.
I'm a-goin' to her—I'm goin'—God bless yer, Jim !
    —good-bye.

ONE WINTER NIGHT.

RAGGED, wretched, worn and weary,
    Come the casuals, creeping in,
    Where the Parish nightly shelters
Shame and sorrow, sloth and sin;
Where the wounded in life's battle,
    Pushed aside and trodden down,
Share the Poor Law's tender mercy
    With the refuse of the town.

When the night has flung her mantle
    Rags and tatters kindly o'er,
Come the outcasts, meekly knocking
    At the black, forbidding door.
All the storm-tossed human wreckage,
    Sport for fortune's changing tide,
Hither drifts as to a harbour—
    Foul and fair float side by side.

Here, through all the long night watches,
    Want and woe can rest their heads :
Who shall say what bygone blisses
    Hover round these narrow beds ?
Stained with travel, bent and broken,
    Here the starving outcast lies,
Yet he smiles—some happy vision
    Sleep has drawn across his eyes.

Sleep has come to weary eyelids,
    Dreams have come to tortured brains,
And in dreams perchance they wander
    Freely o'er life's pleasant plains.
Look where lies a woman sleeping,
    Moaning even in her rest.
With a wee, wan baby pillowed
    On her chill and shrivelled breast.

In her sleep she sees the husband
    Whom the cruel fever slew,
While he sought the honest labour
    He was all too weak to do.
Faint and footsore, broken-hearted,
    Cold and hunger did their work :
Charity that might have saved him
    Went abroad to help the Turk.

When the throes of death were on him,
  With a groan he raised his head,
And he cried, " O God, have mercy
  On my darlings when I'm dead ! "
Then his dying kiss he gave them—
  All that he had left to give—
Still the craved-for mercy tarries,
  For his wife and baby *live*.

         *   *   *

'Tis the Sabbath, and a woman,
  With a baby on her knee,
Sits among the poor who worship
  In the sittings labelled " Free."
From the cutting blast of winter
  She has sought a refuge there,
Though the peasants eye her fiercely,
  Wondering " how such creatures dare."

Rent and ragged are her garments,
  Pinched and pallid is her face ;
She is tramping from the workhouse
  To her distant native place.
Here she rests awhile and listens
  In the warm and cosy church,
While the vicar reads a sermon
  From his velvet-cushioned perch.

For a special sermon chosen
  Is the Saviour's gentle speech,
When He blessed the little children,
  Laying loving hands on each ;
And the parson tells his people
  How God loves the children well,
And will take them to his bosom
  In the golden land to dwell.'

" Dry your eyes," he says, " O mourners,
  When your cherished darlings die ;
Think how warm within God's bosom
  In that happy land they lie.
There no more can pain and anguish
  Wring the heart and cloud the brow —
They are past all sin and sorrow,
  They are happy angels now."

Peals the music of the organ
  As the people pass away ;
O'er the fields they hurry homeward,
  For the skies are ashen grey ;
And a homeless creature totters
  From God's temple with the rest ;
In her heart His loving promise,
  And a baby at her breast.
      *   *   *

Hark, the tempest howls in fury,
  And the snow is falling fast,
As an outcast sinks exhausted,
  For her strength gives way at last.
She is lost upon the moorland,
  Daylight's last faint glimmer fled,
And the shelter that she seeks for
  Lieth weary miles ahead.

She is blinded by the snowstorm,
  And her limbs are numb with cold;
In her rags she wraps the baby
  That her weak arms scarce can hold.
She can feel its frozen body,
  She can hear its piteous cry,
And she thinks as on she staggers,
  What—O God—if she should die!

If her senses should desert her,
  And through all the cruel night
Here her babe should slowly perish—
  Ah, thank God!—she sees a light.
No, her eyes are dim with anguish,
  'Twas a star peeped through a cloud.
Hark, the blast grows fierce and fiercer,
  And the baby moans aloud.

Then the mother clasps it closer,
  While her chill lips press its cheeks;
As her strength comes back a moment,
  In a strange, wild way she speaks :
" Go, O baby dear ! " she murmurs,
  " From my breast, all cold and dry,
Go to where, in God's warm bosom,
  All the happy babies lie."

Pass the preacher's words of comfort
  Swiftly through her tortured brain ;
High above her stretch the heavens
  Where they know not grief and pain.
What had earth to give her baby ?
  What could be its life below?
Just one long, long spell of torture,
  Years of hunger, want, and woe.

Down she kneels, poor maddened mother : —
  God forgive her wicked hand
As it frees a soul, and sends it
  Up to seek the promised land!
Then she leaves her tiny burden,
  All so still and quiet now ;
Stoops to print two loving kisses
  Softly on its marble brow.

        *   *   *

C

Late that night they found her, living,
　And the law condemned her crime.
" Death ! " cried Justice, passing sentence.
　But before the fatal time,
He who took her burden from her
　Flung her prison gates ajar—
He perchance lets tortured mothers
　Pass to where their babies are.

THE MATRON'S STORY.

HE was drunk—mad drunk—was Molly,
the night that I saw her first;
I'd seen some terrible cases, but hers
was the very worst.
This refuge had just been started for the daughters
of night and sin,
And I was the matron here, sir, on the night that
they brought her in.

Her face was flushed and swollen, and a blow had
cut her eye,
And the blood that had oozed unnoticed on her
cheek was caked and dry.
She laughed with a hoarse, wild laughter, and
capered and kicked about,
And she swore and she cursed so foully we thought
we must turn her out.

C 2

She'd come for a spree, as often these poor lost
  creatures come.
They hear of our "midnight meetings" away in
  their filthy slum ;
I've seen 'em jump up on the platform and fling
  down the chairs and shriek,
And join in a ribald chorus when the clergyman
  tried to speak.

But Molly was worse than any—she staggered
  across the place
And picked up a brass-bound hymn-book and aimed
  at our chaplain's face ;
It cut him across the cheek-bone, and he uttered a
  cry of pain,
Then we rushed at Molly to seize her, but she
  struggled with might and main.

She bit and she tore and scratched us, and kicked
  like a beast at bay,
Then all of a sudden reeled forward, and still as a
  mouse she lay ;
In the struggle her wound was injured, and the
  blood flowed down apace,
And the same sort of mark we noticed was on hers
  and the chaplain's face.

What a fist had done for Molly the hymn-book had
    done for him ;
He was only a young beginner, and he trembled in
    every limb ;
For the wound was deep and painful, but he pushed
    his way through the crowd,
And cleared his voice with an effort, and spoke
    these words aloud :

" Poor lass, may the Lord forgive her as I forgive
    her too ! "
And silent, as if by magic, stood the whole of the
    yelling crew;
While he, with his face all bleeding, did the words
    of the Saviour quote,
That the left cheek should be offered to one who
    the right cheek smote.

He came where we held the wanton, and he moved
    his lips in prayer,
And smoothed from her bloody features the masses
    of tangled hair.
" Take her away," he whispered, " and see that her
    wound is drest,"
Then he spake aloud the blessing, and then he dis-
    missed the rest.

We kept the girl at the Refuge right from the hour
    she swooned
Till time and a kindly surgeon had thoroughly
    healed the wound;
In a week it was closed completely, but leaving a
    mark to mar,
And the face of the poor lost creature and *his* had
    the self-same scar.

The day she was well she left us—left us with
    never a word;
Went back to the awful outcasts with whom such
    women herd;
And now and again we gathered news of the life
    she led:
" In the hospital," once they told us, and then that
    the girl was dead.

It was five years after that, sir, one night went our
    faithful priest
On a mission of love and mercy to an awful place
    down East—
To a den where the lowest women herd with the
    vilest thieves—
They're some of the very worst, sir, that our Refuge
    here receives.

He'd heard from a girl who came here tales of this
    Devil's place,
And he made up his mind to storm it, armed with
    the word of Grace.
His face flushed red as he told us, and spoke of the
    souls to win.
And the task that the Lord had set him in that haven
    of shame and sin.

He laughed when we spoke of danger, and that
    night went forth alone,—
But we had a strange misgiving which we hardly
    liked to own ;
He was back on the stroke of midnight—back from
    the jaws of hell,
But his face was pale and ghastly, he'd a strange
    wild tale to tell.

He had entered that filthy alley and spoken God's
    Word aloud,
Till the people swarmed about him in a thick and
    threatening crowd ;
And they jeered and they spat and hooted, and the
    women were worst of all,
For they picked up filth to pelt him, and drove him
    against the wall.

Beaten and bruised and smothered, he then would
    have turned and fled,
When a well-aimed brickbat struck him full on his
    hatless head.
Then he turned quite sick and giddy, and felt himself
    dragged along,
And a door was slammed in the faces of the threat-
    ening, murderous throng.

And beside him there stood a woman—he could
    hardly see her face,
For a foul and a noisome darkness hung o'er the
    dreadful place.
" Hush for your life ! " she whispered, " I've bolted
    and barred the door ;
They'd 'ave your blood if I'd let 'em—hark, how
    the tigers roar !

" They found out as you're the parson as 'tices the
    gals away,
They say it's through you they peaches and goes on
    the ' Christian' lay.
I dragged you in here and saved you, and sent out
    a gal for the slops* ;
Ha, they're a-comin', sir ! Listen ! the noise and
    the shoutin' stops."

---

* The police. The word—originally back slang, " ccilop "—has passed
into the ordinary argot of the street.

The noise was changed in a moment to a hiss and
    a sullen groan,
The woman crept close and listened, then open the
    door was thrown,
And there was a sergeant standing with six of his
    tallest men,
And our chaplain walked between them out of that
    · awful den.

And just as they reached the entry, lo, a woman's
    piercing shriek
Told of the brutal vengeance the ruffians tried to
    wreak.
He guessed what it was, did the sergeant, and hurry-
    ing back they found
The woman who'd saved our chaplain all of a heap
    on the ground.

The crowd in their brutal fury had beaten the
    woman down,
They kicked at her prostrate body till the red blood
    stained her gown ;
But nobody knew who'd done it—the cowards had
    slunk away,
Her face was all white and ghastly in the light of
    the bull's-eye's ray.

'Twas the face of an old acquaintance our chaplain
    saw that night ;
By the scar on the cheek he knew her, in the lantern's
    quivering light—
'Twas Molly, the long lost Molly, the girl that we
    thought was dead—
She beckoned him down and whispered, and these
    were the words she said :

" I know'd yer to-night by yer scar, sir, the scar o'
    the cut I made ;
I heerd how yer treated me then, sir ; how yer give
    me yer blessin' and prayed,
And I sez when I see yer in danger : Moll, you've
    a debt to pay,
So I dragged yer away in yonder, and I 'eld them
    curs at bay."

Died ? No, she didn't ; we saved her—she's matron
    here under me ;
That's she—and ah, here comes the chaplain—now
    both the scars you can see.
And often we tell the story, how the Lord in His
    tender grace
Saved a life and a soul together all through a scar
    on the face.

SIR RUPERT'S WIFE.

 OU see where the cliffs frown yonder in
  a line of dingy red?—
 The wild, fierce crag, the highest, is
  known as Sir Rupert's Head:
It's five hundred feet and over from the brow to
 the sea below,
And it won its name in the winter a hundred years
 ago.
There wasn't a squire in Devon so famous as
 Rupert Leigh;
He was lord of these broad, rich acres, good-
 looking and fancy free.
He came of a race of giants, stood six-feet-two in
 his socks.
And once, for a drunken wager, with his fist he
 had felled an ox.

" Dare-devil Leigh " was his nickname, he was last
of a lawless line
Who had gone to the deuce full gallop, through
women and cards and wine.
He wasn't so bad as they were—he was more of a
hunting squire,
And he freed the name a little from some of the
ancient mire.
His wasn't an easy country, but he'd take it every
inch,
And ride as straight as an arrow where the boldest
well might flinch.
When a lad he had climbed yon headland, climbed
it from base to crest,
For a short-frocked hussy who wanted the eggs
in a seagull's nest.

One winter he went to London—he was then
about forty-three ;
His steward had told the parson he'd lawyers in
town to see.
'Twas dull in the place without him, for his
mansion was Liberty Hall ;
There was always a warm wet welcome for
neighbours who chose to call.

He was gone for a twelvemonth nearly, writing to
    no old friends,
But a Devonshire man in London news to the
    parson sends.
Sir Rupert had married a madam, a play-acting,
    mincing wench,
Who painted and patched and powdered, and was
    finikin, fine, and French.

She was no more French than I am, but this was
    about the time
That French was the title given to nigh every kind
    of crime.
She sang at a minor play-house—in opera, so they
    say—
And he saw her as Polly Peachum in that famous
    work by Gay.
He was always an easy target for a wench's rolling
    eye.
So it got to bouquets and presents, and to letters
    by-and-by.
He was wax in the hussy's fingers, and she moulded
    with practised skill,
Till he took the form of a husband, the slave of her
    slightest will.

They travelled about a little, saw Paris, the Hague,
    and Rome—
Then the news went abroad Sir Rupert was
    bringing his lady home.
The people about here liked him, and no warmth
    did their welcome lack,
But they looked askance at my lady, and she gave
    them their glances back.
They hated her then directly, they chafed at her
    cold disdain,
And they gossiped her story over in language a bit
    too plain.
They called her a " stuck-up stroller," and some-
    how the scandal grew,
Till my lady as " Polly Peachum " the whole of the
    country knew.

Sir Rupert was broken-hearted when he heard of
    the mocking tone,
And he quarrelled with all his comrades until he
    was left alone—
Alone at the Hall with " Polly," for the gentry had
    cut her dead,
But his heart was as true as ever to the woman
    he'd stooped to wed.

To him she was just an angel who'd come from the
holy skies
That his heart might bask for ever in the light of
her lustrous eyes.
No wine, no cards, and no hunting : he kept at my
lady's side—
'Twas a great big boy with a sweetheart, not a man
with a year-won bride.

She pined in the lonely mansion ; she wanted
society—life—
She wanted to play my lady as well as Sir Rupert's
wife.
Sir Rupert must ask a party—not of bumpkins, but
folks from town :
He had plenty of friends in London ; would he not
ask them down ?
They came, and the sound of laughter rang through
the Hall once more,
And my lady was proud and happy, but her
husband's heart was sore ;
He had learned from an idle whisper—a whisper
not meant for him—
A secret that sapped his life-blood and the strength
of each stalwart limb.

He reeled when he heard the whisper and guessed
    at the ghastly truth :
'Twas the tale of a player-woman and a curled and
    scented youth,
A dandy of six-and-twenty, the son of an old, old
    chum—
He was one of the guests invited, and one of the
    first to come.
Sir Rupert had been in London a guest at his
    father's, too,
And this young fop, he remembered, had led him
    his wife to woo ;
He had raved of this Polly Peachum, and dragged
    him to hear her sing ;
He said at the time he knew her—'twas a planned
    and a plotted thing !

And now she was always with him, they chatted
    and laughed away ;
She was cold and dull with Sir Rupert,—with him
    she was kind and gay.
She was weary of playing my lady, of being Sir
    Rupert's wife—
She pined for the tinsel glories of the old
    Bohemian life ;

She hated the dull decorum, she hated the legal
tie—

Her cage was a cage, though gilded. Then the
tempter whispered " Fly! "

One night both their chairs were empty, and slowly
the news leaked out :

Two horses were gone from the stable—'twas a
settled thing, no doubt.

Sir Rupert was white with horror, but he turned to
the gaping crew

And cried, " It's a lie, I tell you !—who dares to say
it's true ? "

Then seizing his holster pistols, he mounted his
fleetest mare

And made straight for the Red Cliff roadway—he
guessed they had gone by there.

For that was the way to London, from Exmouth the
pair would post,

And the road they were bound to travel was the
road by the rugged coast.

If you look you will see it passes right over the
headland's brow—

Only a century distant it wasn't so good as
now.

D

He dug his spurs in the hunter, and it flew up the
    fearful steep.
'Twas a wild, fierce night in the winter, and the
    snow lay thick and deep ;
But the moon through the clouds had broken, and
    right on the Head he spied
A horse that had slipped and fallen, and the rider
    by its side ;
And over them bent a figure, but whose he could
    scarcely see,
Then he uttered a cry to Heaven that his wife
    unharmed might be ;
And lashing his steed to fury, it flew through the
    slippery snow,
While the wild waves roared a warning five
    hundred feet below.

A slip, and both horse and rider would roll to a
    hideous fate,
But Sir Rupert, with set white features, rode to the
    headland straight.
They heard him now, and the woman rose from her
    knees and moaned.
And the man gave a sudden shudder and opened
    his eyes and groaned.

Sir Rupert reined up so fiercely that the mare on
    the precipice reared,
And the woman sprang back with horror, in the
    jaws of the death she feared.
For a moment she seemed to totter, and then with
    a piercing cry
Went over that awful headland that seems to touch
    the sky.

For a second no sound was uttered, only the
    billows roared.
While up from its nest a seagull, startled and
    shrieking, soared ;
Then, shouting for help, Sir Rupert clutched at the
    snow-clad turf,
And glanced with a look of horror down at the
    boiling surf.
And as he lay there peering, right at the farthest
    edge,
Something his eyes detected—a heap on a narrow
    ledge ;
It was thirty feet between them, but he knew 'twas
    his wretched wife,
And he vowed, though his own paid forfeit, he
    would save her guilty life.

He could see there were tiny juttings where his
    foot might find a hold,
And the man he had quite forgotten was worth his
    weight in gold.
The booby was bruised and shaken, and fancied
    that he should die,
But Sir Rupert bade him help him or he'd shoot
    him by-and-by.
Then the white-faced coward whimpered and lifted
    his jewelled hands,
And Sir Rupert set him tearing his mantle in
    narrow bands.
Then the strips were twined together and tied to a
    rough stone seat,
And over went brave Sir Rupert, clinging with
    hands and feet.

The waves in their winter fury shrieked for a
    human life,
But down and down crept Rupert till he swung by
    his senseless wife.
Stooping, he clasped her firmly, one hand on the
    doubtful rope,
Pressed his lips on her marble forehead, and
    whispered her, " Darling—hope ! "

Then breathing a prayer to Heaven to save them
both that night,
He toiled with his heavy burden up the face of the
frowning height.
A fall of the soft red sandstone, a slip of his
bleeding hand,
And their bodies had lain together, crushed on the
cruel strand.

Safe! safe at last on the summit! safe on the firm
hard road! ·
There where the moonbeams glittered, he glanced
at his senseless load.
Her face was bruised and battered, and the warm
blood welled and gushed ;
And he saw that his wife was injured, and her
tender bones were crushed.   ·
No trace of the lady's gallant ; he'd limped to a
horse and flown :
Sir Rupert and "Polly Peachum" were there on
the heights alone.
He leaped on the gallant hunter, took his wife in
his brawny arms,
And galloped across the country to one of his
tenants' farms.

For six long months my lady hovered 'twixt death
and life—
'Twas a surgeon who came from London that
saved Sir Rupert's wife—
And when she was out of danger it was known she
was marked and maimed—
A battered, misshapen cripple, distorted and scarred
and lamed.
But Sir Rupert clung closer to her, they travelled
from place to place,
And he never winced or shuddered at the sight of
her injured face.
It was he who carried the cripple, who nursed her
with tenderest care :
And never in knightly story such gallant had lady
fair.

For many a year she lingered—'twas up at the Hall
she died,
And here in the village churchyard they're sleeping
side by side.
She died in his arms confessing the worth of his
noble love,
And in less than a year he sought her in the
mansions of God above.

There stands the great bluff headland—there swells
    the sea below—
And the story I've told you happened nigh a
    hundred years ago.
Yet there isn't a soul that visits those towering
    crags of red
But thinks of the love and daring that hallowed
    "Sir Rupert's Head."

A CHRISTMAS STORY.

THEY quarrelled on Christmas night,
    Fell out, and it came to blows.
  No! it wasn't a stand-up fight;
For the woman was one of those
Who love like a faithful dog,
    With a love as deep as mute.
Will was primed with the Christmas grog,
    And drunk he was just a brute.

A wee frail thing was she,
    A trembling, pale-faced wench;
And a burly chap was he,
    With a giant's fist to clench.
He clenched it that night with rage
    At something his help-meet said ;--
Some counsel discreet and sage—
    It was that to the quarrel led.

It was but a loving word,
    Just a thrifty wife's advice ;
She wasn't a scold to gird,
    But his wrath was up in a trice.
He was always a hasty chap,
    And quick with a word and blow ;
If he hadn't been drunk, mayhap,
    Things wouldn't have happened so.

He up with his fist, did Will,
    And he hit her across the head—
She groaned, and then all was still,
    And she lay like a lump of lead.
She had fallen across the chair,
    And her face was white as death ;
He opened the door for air,
    And listened to hear her breath.

He looked in her ashen face
    And saw where his fist had hit—
Near the temple—a nasty place—
    And the skin with the blow had split.
Down on his knees he fell,
    Sobered and shaking now ;
In his heart he had loved her well,
    And it was but a drunken row.

Dead!—not a sign of life,
  Not a flutter—he strained his ears;
He gazed on his murdered wife
  With a thousand ghastly fears.
His brain was aflame.   He thought
  Of the murderer's awful doom;
Safety in flight he sought,
  And rushed from the haunted room.

He wandered and wandered far
  Away from the ghastly sight,
Seeing in every star
  God's eye on that Christmas night.
With her wraith at his heels he flew,
  Travelled and sought the sea,
And, joining a rabble crew,
  Sailed for the wild West free.

Over the whole earth's face,
  Bearing the brand of Cain—
Now in some savage place,
  Now on the distant main—
Wandered the guilty wretch,
  Haunted by night and day,
With his hands too foul to stretch
  Up to the skies and pray.

Haggard and worn and weak,
  Men read in his deep-lined brow
A story he dared not speak,
  And all of them shunned him now.
Outcast, with never a friend
  Under the world-wide sky,
Longed he his life to end,
  Yet did he fear to die.

Accursed of God he bore
  The weight of a voiceless woe
Till the years he counted as four
  Since he struck the fatal blow.
And the Christmas time came round
  As they sighted a famous strand,
Where Old England's sons have found
  A home in a foreign land.

There the bells rang out a chime
  On the sultry Christmas morn,
To tell of the sweet glad time
  When Christ the Lord was born.
They rang in the outcast's ears
  A message of tender love;
Then, his face all wet with tears,
  He prayed to the God above.

And when from his knees he rose
　　There was hope in the sinner's breast;
He had seen how his life should close—
　　God had pointed the path to rest.
Homeward he bent his way,
　　Home to the far-off goal,
To tell in the light of day
　　The secret that seared his soul.

　　　　*　　　*　　　*

Ah! weary the road has been,
　　But the pilgrim stands at last
There on the old, old scene,
　　There with the ghastly past.
He will see where he struck the blow
　　Ere he goes to his righteous fate,
And then shall grim justice know
　　Who knocks at her iron gate.

He will whisper his secret then
　　That is known but to God on high;
It soon shall be known of men—
　　What will it cost to die?
'Twas God, when he prayed, who lent
　　Peace to his tortured breast,
By Him was the pilgrim sent
　　That confession his soul might rest.

He stands in the early morn
   There, where the deed was done,
Just as the light is born
   Of the faint December sun.
He peers in the tiny room,
   Then reels with a scared white face—
Is it part of his awful doom
   That *her* ghost shall haunt the place?

There!—there on the cursed spot!—
   " Mercy, O God!" he cries;
And his breath comes fast and hot—
   How she stares with those sweet blue eyes!
She comes down the garden walk
   With her arms outstretched to him;
Can a phantom in daylight stalk
   As it does in the twilight dim?

She comes, and he tries to scream,
   " Back! phantom of flesh and blood!"
'Tis a murderer's ghastly dream;
   Yet hark, how her heart goes thud!
It is she! 'Tis his winsome wife!
   No ghost from a noisome tomb;
Her kiss has the warmth of life,—
   He is saved from a murderer's doom.

Hark, how the bells ring out
 Sweet on the frosty air ;
God's message—ah ! never a doubt —
 " Behold how I answer prayer."
Told is the story soon
 How she whom he fancied dead
Had come from her death-like swoon
 Only to find him fled.

" He has left me," she thought, and wept.
 " He has left me for evermore ! "
Yet true had her fond heart kept
 As slowly the years passed o'er.
It is Noel, the glad bells say,
 As they clang from the steeple's height ;
Let the joy of this Christmas Day
 Atone for that Christmas night.

A SILVER WEDDING.

"TO Dick on our silver wedding, from
       Harold and Elspeth Grey "—
Give me my glasses, nephew.   Is that
       what the letters say ?
How stiffly these lockets open.   Ah, there's a spring,
       I see,
A picture of both, God bless them ! to show that
       they think of me.
Did ever you see two faces so sweet and calm and
       kind ?
Their ocean of life can hardly have known a
       boisterous wind.
Look at their happy features—the peace in the
       eyes of each—
Ah, strange is the tale they'd tell you had pictures
       the gift of speech.

To-day is their silver wedding—a fourth of a
    century's past
Since, after a fierce, wild tempest, they came to
    their rest at last ;
And I who had known their story, who from boy-
    hood had been *his* friend,
Knelt with them both at the altar where their lives
    were to meet and blend.
But a year was gone and over since their names
    were asked in church,
And whispers went round the neighbours so ready
    one's fame to smirch.
The wedding was fixed and settled, the wedding
    that should have been—
But it happened a twelvemonth later—the first one
    was stopped, I mean.

Yes, stopped, as it were, at the altar, stopped on
    the very morn,
And the bride had to hide her secret, and swallow
    the whispered scorn.
She was dressed in her bridal raiment, and bonny
    and flushed and glad,
When he came to the house like a spectre, with a
    look so scared and mad

That the bridesmaids shook like aspens as he
    passed them in the hall.
Then he asked for the mother and Elspeth, and
    then came a cry and fall—
She had fainted away, poor darling. He had left
    it till the last,
This message of evil fortune, that came like a
    blighting blast.

And presently Elspeth's father came, with a stern-
    set face,
To gather the guests together, all who were in the
    place.
He said that a great misfortune had come upon
    Harold Grey,
And his daughter was lying speechless, and would
    be no bride that day.
Then the guests in their wedding favours drove fast
    from the scene of grief;
And I went away to St. Peter's with a message as
    strange as brief.
I whispered the waiting clergy, and passed to the
    crowded pews,
Telling her friends and kinsfolk the sad and
    mysterious news.

"To Dick on our silver wedding "—I was always
  his old friend Dick;
We were chums when the oats were sowing and the
  pulse of our youth beat quick.
We were students in Paris together, we were both
  of us mad for art,
We lodged in the Latin Quarter, and for months
  were never apart,   .
Till Harold got hit by a model, a beautiful, bold,
  bad girl,
With a face that was meant for mischief and eyes
  to set brains in a whirl.
She angled for Harold, the hussy, and landed him
  safe ashore;
He married the jade, poor fellow, and then we were
  chums no more.

His father had left him money, and Harold was well
  to do,
He gave up the Latin Quarter and the old Bohemian
  crew,
And taking his Mimi with him went back to his
  English home,
And then, so I heard from his cousin, he went
  painting again to Rome.

From time to time still I gathered some news of
his wandering life—
He was worried and ill, they told me, and had work
with his foreign wife.
She left him at last in a passion—left him and
crossed the seas,
And his lawyers sent her monthly, the price of
their client's ease.

Then Harold and I were cronies once more as in
days gone by,
For he sought me out in my chambers, and told me
with many a sigh
Of the bonds that had worn his heart out, and how,
now that his life was free,
He had thought of our old, sweet friendship, and
how happy he'd been with me;
Here we had rooms together and painted and
smoked and wrote,
Contented on life's vast ocean like rudderless ships
to float.
We were happy as lords and as lazy, when a
message to Harold came
That the Court of Death had divorced him from the
woman who bore his name.

Two years went by ere he whispered a secret he'd
    kept with care—
A story all love and rapture, and the charms of a
    maiden fair.
He spoke of his boyhood's error and his manhood's
    bitter pain,
And the angel who'd come to bless him, the beau-
    tiful Elspeth Rayne.
It was settled before he told me, and they'd fixed
    the happy day—
I must see her at once; he took me and carried me
    straight away
To papa and mamma and Elspeth, and I felt such an
    awkward stick
When Harold, his blue eyes laughing, cried, "This
    is my dear old Dick!"

He spoke of our life-long friendship, and how good
    I had been to him,
Till I felt like a blushing schoolgirl and my eyes
    were queer and dim;
And his Elspeth came and whispered, she feared I
    should hate her *so*—
I was one of the family circle, like a friend of the
    long ago.

Well, the time came round for the wedding, and the
    night before we met,
And we spoke of the glad to-morrow—ah, that
    night I shall ne'er forget !
I and Harold went home together, our path lay by
    Thames's tide,
And he spoke of the dead that evening, and then
    of to-morrow's bride.

And just by the bridge a woman passed us with
    lightning speed,
In a moment we guessed her errand, in a second
    she did the deed ;
A cry on the cold black waters, then a leap from
    the muddy strand,
Brave Harold had plunged and seized her and had
    dragged her safe to land.
The people had come about us, and a hearty cheer
    was raised ;
But *he* with a look of horror in the face of the out-
    cast gazed,
For there, with her breast fast heaving with the
    signs of returning life,
Lay the woman he once had honoured with the
    sacred name of wife.

Her death was a well-planned fiction—she nourished
    a cruel hate,
And bided her time to strike him, on the eve of a
    happier fate.
She would wait till he wedded another, then prey
    on his hopes and fears,
And the gold that would buy her silence would pay
    for the two lost years.
But she drank, and her brain was maddened; she
    had leapt in the stream to-night
When her soul was a prey to terrors and the fever
    was at its height.
He bore her away and housed her, and hid her from
    prying eyes,
And the limbs of the law came slowly to find they
    had lost their prize.

When the shock Time's hand had softened, came
    beautiful Elspeth Rayne
To kneel by the side of the woman, who moaned
    with a ceaseless pain ;
She prayed to the God of mercy to spare the poor
    lost soul,
The time to repent her trespass and strive for the
    heavenly goal.

And never a sign made Harold of the broken
    heart within,
For he smothered his love for Elspeth as a black
    and an awful sin ;
But she, like a noble woman, came here as the
    outcast's friend,
And nursed her with me and Harold right to the
    very end.

One eve, as the shadows deepened, and we sat by
    the patient's bed,
She spoke, in her broken English, and asked us to
    raise her head ;
She called to her spouse and Elspeth to stand in
    the fading light,   ·
That her eyes might rest on their faces and be
    blessed with the holy sight ;
Then, taking their hands, she joined them, and
    bade them forgive her sin,
And pray to the Lord of Heaven to pity and take
    her in ;
" And when I am dead," she murmured, " let
    Elspeth be your bride " ;
Then she spoke no more till the morrow, when she
    blessed them both and died.

"To Dick on our silver wedding." They know that
  I've got the gout—
They know I'd have been amongst them if the
  doctors would let me out—
And down in the sweet green country, where their
  happy lives have flown,
They can picture these grimy chambers, where I
  grumble and growl alone.
And to-day is their silver wedding—I look at each
  handsome face,
There's never a look less tender, and never a
  vanished grace—
Give me that bottle, nephew—a fig for what
  doctors say !—
Gout or no gout, here's a bumper to Harold and
  Elspeth Grey !

A LAST LOOK.

I heard him, Joe, I heard him —
    I heard the doctor say
My sight was growing weaker,
    And failing day by day.
" She's going blind," he whispered ;
    Yes, darling, it is true ;
These eyes will soon have taken
    Their last long look at you.

The room is dull and misty,
    And as I try to gaze
There seems to fall between us
    A thick and cruel haze.
I'm going blind, my darling ;
    Ah ! soon the day must be
When these poor eyes will open,
    And vainly try to see.

Oh, take my hand, my husband,
　　To lead me to the light,
And let your dear face linger
　　The last thing in my sight—
That so I may remember,
　　When darkness covers all,
'Twas there I last saw, softly,
　　God's blessed sunshine fall.

Cheer up, my dear old sweetheart,
　　And brush away your tears,
The look I see to-day, love,
　　Will linger through the years.
For when the veil has fallen,
　　To hide you evermore,
I want your smile to light me
　　Along the gloomy shore.

I yet can see you, darling—
　　Some light there lingers still;
The sun is setting slowly
　　Behind the distant hill;
Odd fancies crowd about me
　　Now God has let me know
My eyes must close for ever
　　On all things here below.

Though twenty years have vanished,
   It seems but yestere'en
Since first you wooed and won me
   Among the meadows green ;
Here from our cottage window
   I once could see the spot
Where grew the yellow cowslip
   And blue forget-me-not.

But now a strange mist hovers,
   And though I strain my eyes,
Beyond my yearning glances
   The dear old meadow lies.
I want to see it, darling,
   The meadow by the stream,
Where first your loving whisper
   Fulfilled my girlhood's dream.

So take my hand and guide me,
   And lead me to the air,—
I want to see the world, love,
   That God has made so fair.
I want to see the sunset,
   · And look upon the sky,
And bid the sweet, green country
   A loving, last good-bye !

How swift the sun is setting !
　It's almost twilight now ;
I hear, but cannot see, dear,
　The birds upon the bough.
Is this our little garden ?
　I cannot pierce the gloom,
But I can smell the roses—
　They're coming into bloom.

Stoop down and pluck a rosebud—
　You know my fav'rite tree ;
My husband's hand will give me
　The last one I shall see.
Ah, Joe, do you remember
　The dear old happy days—
Our love among the roses
　In summer's golden blaze ?

I take the rose you give me,
　Its petals damp with dew ;
I scent its fragrant odour,
　But scarce can see its hue.
In memory of to-night, Joe,
　When dead I'll keep it still ;
The rose may fade and wither—
　Our love, dear, never will.

Quick! Quick! my footsteps falter;
  Oh, take me in again;
I cannot bear the air, Joe,
  My poor eyes feel the strain.
Home, home, and bring my children,
  And place them at my knee,
And let me look upon them
  While yet I've time to see.

Then take them gently from me,
  And let us be alone:
My last fond look, dear husband,
  Must be for you alone.
You've been my dear old sweetheart
  Since we were lass and lad:
I've laughed when you were merry,
  And wept when you were sad.

I want to see you wearing
  Your old sweet smile to-night.
I want to take it with me
  To make my darkness light.
God bless you, Joe, for trying—
  Yes, that's the dear old look!
I'll think of that sweet story
  When God has closed the book.

Joe, fetch me down the picture
  That hangs beside our bed.
Ah, love, do you remember
  The day that he lay dead?
Our first-born bonny baby—
  And how we sat and cried,
And thought our hearts were broken
  When our sweet darling died?

I'd like to see the picture
  Once more, dear, while I may,
Though in my heart it lingers
  As though 'twere yesterday.
Ah ! many bairns came after,
  But none were like to him.
Come closer to me, darling,
  The light is growing dim.

Come closer—so ; and hold me,
  And press your face to mine.
I'm in a land of shadows,
  Where ne'er a light can shine.
But with your arm around me,
  What danger need I fear?
I'll never need my eyes, Joe,
  While your strong arm is near.

          *   *   *

Now, be a brave old darling,
  And promise not to fret ;
I saw your face the last, dear,
  And now I've no regret.
I saw your face the last, dear—
  God's hand has dealt the blow ;
My sight went out at sunset
  A short half-hour ago.

Now you must be my eyesight,
  Through all the sunless land,
And down life's hill we'll wander,
  Like lovers, hand in hand.
Till God shall lift the curtain
  Beyond these realms of pain ;
And there, where blind eyes open,
  I'll see your face again.

THE EARL'S DAUGHTER.

HE stood beside the smiling stream that
    mirrored back her face,
And seemed to say, "Oh weary one,
    behold thy resting place!"
The rippling water kissed her feet, and murmured,
    "Daughter, rest;
Come lie as in a mother's arms, and sleep upon my
    breast."

The river sang its lullaby; her eyelids, drooping
    down,
Let fall their fringèd curtains o'er her eyes of hazel
    brown—
The sweet brown eyes that looking back beheld the
    cloud of shame,
And all her life's wild history writ out in words of
    flame.

In sin those brown eyes saw the light, but sin of
    high degree ;
The daughter of an English earl of noble blood
    was she.
In strange weird ways by Fate's big loom our web
    of fortune 's spun,
And *she* was doomed when Phryne's face my lord's
    allegiance won.

A player wench she had for dam, who made the
    stage a mart,
And reared an altar high to vice within the fane of
    art ;
She sinned and played, and played to sin—a bold
    and brazen girl
Who won—and kept, so rumour says, for three whole
    years the earl.

And Nell, the baby, had his eyes, and he would
    kiss the child ;
And when folks praised her pretty face, he looked
    at her and smiled.
But earls have worlds so wide to roam in search of
    noble joys,
He found fresh playthings by and by and left his
    early toys.

He sowed his oats and settled down, and took a
noble dame,
And had a daughter born to him to bear her father's
name ;
The player wench was pensioned off, and Nell was
pensioned too :
He washed his hands of wicked things, and started
life anew.

A cheque was drawn—a good round sum—and Nell's
next nurse was one
Who'd sit with her the livelong day—a viscount's
eldest son ;
But by and by, as Nellie grew too old to romp
and play,
The mother found a growing girl was sometimes
in the way.

She cowed the child and called her "brat"; her
presence was a tie ;
And when poor Nell was ill and weak half hoped
that she would die ;
The good round sum the earl had paid, "in full of
every claim,"
Was long since spent, but Nell remained poor child
of sin and shame.

The years passed on, and Nell was put to shift
    as best she could ;
The mother thought the stage might lead her child
    to something good ;
She stood half draped in loose burlesques, and
    blushed and lost her head,
And trembled when the men came round, and burst
    in tears and fled.

Then Phryne cursed the weeping Nell, and bade
    her pack and go,
And in her passion hit the girl a foul and cruel
    blow,
That woke the evil passions there ; the slumbering
    devil rose,
That night three lovers came to woo ; she listened
    and she chose.

            *   *   *

To end her sinful life to-day she seeks the waters
    deep,
A gnawing hunger in her heart to close her eyes and
    sleep.
Too proud to cheat and rob and lie, her wings are
    broken soon ;
The evening shadows cross her path ere yet it
    should be noon.

She stands beside the stream that laves an earl's
    far reaching ground;
She hears a voice, and peers between the hedge
    that runs around;
Then turns away, and cries, "O God! had such a
    lot been mine,
I had not e'er been forced to sin, and break Thy
    laws divine."

Within the grounds a father sat beside his daughter
    fair,
And fondly pressed his lips to hers and smoothed
    her glossy hair;
A world of love was in her eyes, as in her girlish
    glee
She flung her arms about his neck and rested on
    his knee.

*   *   *

That eve the river, flinging back the sunset's ruby
    glow,
Bore gently on its glassy breast a sleeper to and
    fro;
It left its burden near *his* grounds, and there, while
    still it lay,
His daughter saw the dreadful sight, and screamed
    and turned away.

He clasped her close and soothed her fears, then
    bade his menials go—
How dared they let a wretched corpse upset his
    darling so !
' Go float it down," the earl exclaimed. " and leave
    it in the shed ;
Then bid the parish people come and fetch away
    their dead."

He left her living, spurned her dead ; his blood was
    in her veins ;
He sinned, and all her weary life *she* wore the
    felon's chains ;
But in the great Recorder's Book, where Nell's
    black life is shown,
Against her sins a righteous Judge will put *his*
    name alone.

OSTLER JOE.

I STOOD at eve, as the sun went down, by a grave where a woman lies,
Who lured men's souls to the shores of sin with the light of her wanton eyes,
Who sang the song that the Siren sang on the treacherous Lurley height,
Whose face was as fair as a summer day, and whose heart was as black as night.

Yet a blossom I fain would pluck to-day from the garden above her dust;
Not the languorous lily of soulless sin nor the blood-red rose of lust;
But a sweet white blossom of holy love' that grew in the one green spot
In the arid desert of Phryne's life, where all was parched and hot.

*   *   *

In the summer, when the meadows were aglow
   with blue and red,
Joe, the ostler of the Magpie, and fair Annie Smith
   were wed.
Plump was Annie, plump and pretty, with a check
   as white as snow;
He was anything but handsome was the Magpie's
   ostler, Joe.

But he won the winsome lassie.   They'd a cottage
   and a cow,
And her matronhood sat lightly on the village
   beauty's brow.
Sped the months and came a baby—such a blue-
   eyed baby boy!
Joe was working in the stables when they told him
   of his joy.

He was rubbing down the horses, and he gave
   them then and there
All a special feed of clover, just in honour of the
   heir:
It had been his great ambition, and he told the
   horses so,
That the Fates would send a baby who might bear
   the name of Joe.

Little Joe the child was christened, and, like
    babies, grew apace ;
He'd his mother's eyes of azure and his father's
    honest face.
Swift the happy years went over, years of blue and
    cloudless sky ;
Love was lord of that small cottage, and the
    tempests passed them by.

Passed them by for years, then swiftly burst in
    fury o'er their home.
Down the lane by Annie's cottage chanced a
    gentleman to roam ;
Thrice he came and saw her sitting by the window
    with her child,
And he nodded to the baby, and the baby laughed
    and smiled.

So at last it grew to know him—little Joe was
    nearly four ;
He would call the ' pretty gemplun' as he passed
    the open door ;
And one day he ran and caught him, and in child's
    play pulled him in,
And the baby Joe had prayed for brought about the
    mother's sin.

'Twas the same old wretched story that for ages
  bards have sung :
'Twas a woman weak and wanton and a villain's
  tempting tongue ;
'Twas a picture deftly painted for a silly creature's
  eyes
Of the Babylonian wonders and the joy that in
  them lies.

Annie listened and was tempted ; she was tempted
  and she fell,
As the angels fell from heaven to the blackest
  depths of hell ;
She was promised wealth and splendour and a
  life of guilty sloth,
Yellow gold for child and husband,—and the
  woman left them both.

Home one eve came Joe the Ostler with a cheery
  cry of ' Wife ! '
Finding that which blurred for ever all the story of
  his life.
She had left a silly letter,—through the cruel scrawl
  he spelt ;
Then he sought the lonely bed-room, joined his
  horny hands and knelt.

" Now, O Lord, O God, forgive her, for she ain't to
    blame !" he cried ;
" For I owt t'a seen her trouble, and 'a gone away
    and died.
Why, a wench like her—God bless her !—'twasn't
    likely as her'd rest
With that bonny head for ever on a ostler's ragged
    vest.

"It was kind o' her to bear me all this long and
    happy time,
So for my sake please to bless her, though You
    count her deed a crime ;
If so be I don't pray proper, Lord, forgive me ; for
    You see
I can talk all right to 'osses, but I'm nervous like
    with Thee."

Ne'er a line came to the cottage from the woman
    who had flown ;
Joe the baby died that winter, and the man was
    left alone.
Ne'er a bitter word he uttered, but in silence
    kissed the rod,
Saving what he told his horses, saving what he
    told his God.

Far away in mighty London rose the woman into
    fame,
For her beauty won men's homage, and she
    prospered in her shame;
Quick from lord to lord she flitted, higher still each
    prize she won,
And her rivals paled beside her as the stars beside
    the sun.

Next she made the stage her market, and she
    dragged Art's temple down
To the level of a show place for the outcasts of the
    town.
And the kisses she had given to poor Ostler Joe for
    nought
With their gold and costly jewels rich and titled
    lovers bought.

Went the years with flying footsteps while her star
    was at its height;
Then the darkness came on swiftly, and the
    gloaming turned to night.
Shattered strength and faded beauty tore the
    laurels from her brow;
Of the thousands who had worshipped never one
    came near her now.

Broken down in health and fortune, men forgot her
  very name,
Till the news that she was dying woke the echoes
  of her fame;
And the papers in their gossip mentioned how an
  "actress" lay
Sick to death in humble lodgings, growing weaker
  every day.

One there was who read the story in a far-off
  country place,
And that night the dying woman woke and looked
  upon his face.
Once again the strong arms clasped her that had
  clasped her long ago,
And the weary head lay pillowed on the breast of
  Ostler Joe.

All the past had he forgotten, all the sorrow and the
  shame;
He had found her sick and lonely, and his wife he
  now could claim.
Since the grand folks who had known her once and
  all had slunk away,
He could clasp his long-lost darling, and no man
  would say him nay.

In his arms death found her lying, in his arms her
    spirit fled ;
And his tears came down in torrents as he knelt
    beside her dead.
Never once his love had faltered through her base
    unhallowed life ;
And the stone above her ashes bears the honoured
    name of wife.

*   *   *

That's the blossom I fain would pluck to-day from
    the garden above her dust;
Not the languorous lily of soulless sin nor the blood-
    red rose of lust ;
But a sweet white blossom of holy love that grew
    in the one green spot
In the arid desert of Phryne's life, where all was
    parched and hot.

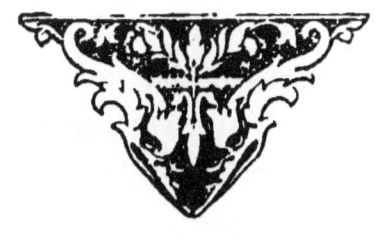

BEAUTY AND THE BEAST.

HARK! It is over! The organ peals,
    The Bishop has mumbled the final word
    Over the chancel the sunlight steals,
  Mocking the sob the bridesmaids heard.
Here, in the sight of a God above,
    A Lord has taken a fair young bride;
Here they have sworn to honour and love,
    And each of them knew that the other lied.

This is a market where slaves are sold;
    Rare is the slave that they sell to-day.
They barter her sweet white flesh for gold
    To a noble sheep who has gone astray.
For rank and jewels and vast estates
    They forced his badge on her dainty hand,
Sealing her doom to the worst of fates—
    Here in a church in a Christian land.

My lord the Bishop, he bowed his head,
　And rolled his eyes with a mellowed grace,
As the beautiful words in the book he read,
　And a sunbeam fell on his saintly face—
His lordship knew of the bridegroom's fame—
　He knew of the women, the cards, and wine ;
But up from the altar he sent his name
　To be specially blessed by the King divine.

He gazed on the face of the high-born maid,
　And saw the mark where the tears had been ;
He knew that a daughter had wept and prayed,
　He knew that a mother had feared a scene—
Had torn herself from the weeping girl,
　Whose love was away o'er the distant sea,
And had sold her child to a titled churl
　Who had just got round from a bad *d. t.*

Back from the doors with the ragged crew !
　Line the passage on either side !
Hide her shame from the people's view !
　Hurry her off, the trembling bride !
There isn't a man in the motley crowd
　But knows of her owner's evil life ;
And they tell the tale of his sins aloud,
　Till the wantons pity the new-made wife.

The air is gay with the wedding chimes,
    Over the town the news they tell,
That a Bishop has blessed the worst of crimes,
    And now they are tolling a maiden's knell.
His lordship follows his dainty prize;
    Now whip the horses, and speed away!
Look at the tears in her swollen eyes—
    Pity, my lord, for your helpless prey!

          *   *   *

Over the seas on a barbarous coast,
    A soldier leads in a desperate fight
A handful of men 'gainst a swarming host,
    And the battle is waged from dawn till night.
One to a hundred still they stand,
    Fighting like heroes, and win at last;
And the news goes home to the distant land,
    And his fame is spread with a trumpet-blast.

She hears the story a week new wed,
    For his gallant deed is on every tongue;
Oft for him have her prayers been said,
    Oft for him have her hands been wrung.
He was the hero she loved so long,
    His was the image that filled her heart;,
Ah, she had done him a grievous wrong!
    Well, it was best they were leagues apart.

She thought of the soldier who fought so well,
   And then of the *roue* whose rings she wore ;
She hears the tales that the gossips tell
   Of the evil life that he led before.
She hears the tales and she doubts them not,
   For once again he has broken out ;
He comes to his couch like a drunken sot,
   And leaves strange letters and *cartes* about.

What does it matter one jot to her ?
   Let him go to the bad at his own mad pace ;
No word she spoke would her lord deter ;
   He'd laugh with scorn in her pleading face.
She winced but once—at the season's height
   A creature sat by her husband's side,
And drove the ponies in all men's sight
   His friends had given the new-made bride.

Never a flush on her marble brow,
   Only a curl of her faultless lip ;
The world's tongue wags with the story now,
   And her lord goes off on a lengthy trip.
All men pity, and some of them speak,
   And sigh o'er the wrongs of the reigning belle ;
The papers have paragraphs week by week,
   And wider and wider the scandals swell.

                G

Her *carte* is hung in the West-end shops,
    With her name in full on the white below;
And all day long there's a big crowd stops
    To look at the lady who's " all the go."
Queen is she of her set to-day,
    In the realms of fashion she reigns alone ;—
She should hear what the coarse-tongued rabble say,
    Now the price she paid for her name is known.

And not alone do the rabble speak ;
    There's something Society whispers too—
It was all the talk of the Ascot week :
    The scandal's delightfully fresh and new.
The lover who went to the wars is back—
    Back with the fame which his sword had won ;
And of more than malice the stories smack
    That round on the lips of the gossips run.

Wherever is Venus, there is Mars.
    Her face lights up when he comes about—
Ascot gave matter for spiteful " pars "
    And Henley has put it beyond a doubt.
Her love shines out through her splendid eyes ;
    Love is a passion, or right or wrong :
Pity the woman who wildly tries
    To stem a torrent, yet floats along.

Gaze on the photo of " Beauty " hung—
  Hung in the shops for cads to buy.
Little you dream how her heart is wrung,
  Little you dream how that breast can sigh.
Let us think of the Turk with a feeling heart,
  Who sells his slaves in the wanton East ;
Here we have mothers who hold a mart,
  And " Beauty " is sold to the wealthy "Beast."

A LEGEND OF LOVE.

IS it true, this dainty story ?
  Is it true—ah, who shall say ?
 In the brighter noonday glory
  Morning shadows melt away.
Poets' fancies woven gaily,
  Cruel fingers tear apart ;
And in judgment Brain sits daily
  On the children of the heart.

Is it true ?   O bid defiance
  To the doubters' cruel eyes—
Men who take as toys of science
  All the glories of the skies.
Better far the foolish savage
  Who on twenty Gods will call,
Than the scholar doubts can ravage,
  Till he knows no God at all.

*   *   *

O'er the leagues of stormy water
   Came a story on the breeze;
From a cruel field of slaughter
   It was borne across the seas.
'Mid the roar of mighty Babel
   It was whispered far and wide;
'Twas a tearful tender fable
   Of a hero who had died.

Years ago, in times called olden—
   'Tis a legend, mind, I tell—
From his throne, high reared and golden,
   Cast to earth, a ruler fell.
Fought by foreign foes and worsted,
   Mad with grief, and mad with shame,
For his blood the people thirsted,
   And heaped curses on his name.

Far away, an exile broken,
   Shorn of all his pomp and pride,
Cæsar passed his race's token
   To his only son; and died.
Died afar, by all unheeded
   Who of yore had bent the knee;
And he sleeps the sleep he needed
   In his tomb across the sea.

To that son the right descended
    Still to count himself a king;
Courtiers still his steps attended,
    Doubting not what time would bring;
And he kept the grand tradition
    Of his proud Imperial race:
" Bide your time," was Cæsar's mission;
    " You shall fill your father's place."

Yet the waves of time they bore him
    Little nearer to the throne:
Blood, he said, should not restore him,
    But his people's love alone.
Not for him the pathway gory,
    That his hero-fathers trod;
He would keep his whole life-story
    Fit for eyes of man and God.

So he grew among the strangers
    Till he came to man's estate,
Then he sought afar the dangers
    That beset a soldier's fate.
Why? Ah, whisper, gentle breezes,
    Ye that come across the sea,
With the tender tale it pleases
    Cruel Fate to send by thee!

He had loved a high-born maiden,
  Youngest daughter of a Queen;
Yet his heart with grief was laden—
  Shadows crept their loves between.
Fancy cast a dream-spell o'er him;
  Then the ghosts of history came—
Spread his race's past before him,
  While in blood they wrote his name.

Lines of upraised daggers gleaming,
  Pointed ever at his heart;
Crowned at last, though in his dreaming,
  He was playing Cæsar's part.
Then he clasped his queen, to save her
  From the mob who sought her life;
Just one wild embrace he gave her;
  And then fell the fatal knife.

Back he thrust the dream appalling,
  While with ashen face he swore
He would list to duty's calling,
  But would think of love no more.
Down he crushed his hope for ever,
  Shunned the maiden's tender eyes;
Hearts were wrung in that endeavour—
  Tears would all unbidden rise.

One short word had he but spoken,
  His had been the maiden's hand;
In her eyes he read the token,
  He could see the promised land.
Love that's checked is love the stronger;
  Should he bid her be his mate?
God forbid that he should wrong her!
  She should know a happier fate.

He was heir to pomp and splendour;
  Hope might dawn for him at last;
Fiercest foes might yet surrender:
  But the fatal die was cast.
Comes his dirge across the billows;
  Sets his gentle star for aye.
Death his crownless head now pillows—
  He has flung his life away.

Came a whisper o'er the ocean,
  He had sought a soldier's death;
And to seal a life's devotion,
  Gave *her* land his latest breath.
Reckless there he courted danger—
  And the tale is far and wide,
How the youth, to fear a stranger,
  Death had wooed and won for bride.
          *   *   *

Is it true, this legend olden,
  Or some poet's idle dream,
Who has sought, in garments golden,
  Thus to dress a dainty theme?
If aright they tell his story,
  All his race he soars above;
They are men who die for glory,
  'Twas a god who died for love.

FORGOTTEN—A LAST INTERVIEW.

HARLEY, I'm glad to see you! I
thought you'd forgotten me quite;
It's rarely I see an actor, and it's always
a welcome sight.
And how goes the show this Christmas? You're
making a name, I see;
Does anyone ever wonder and ask what's become
of me?
There, don't nod your head to please me; why, it's
years since I left the stage;
Five years, at the least, old fellow—I'm one of a
bygone age.
And, lying here sick and weary, and worn with the
ceaseless pain,
I wonder if folks remember my seasons at Drury
Lane.

Whenever the Lane tried Shakespeare, I was one
    of the leading men ;
You saw me as Hamlet, Charley, the night that I
    had my Ben.
I was reckoned a fairish actor, and the public liked
    me well,
Though, maybe, they'd call me stagey, now Shake-
    speare must suit the swell.
But then I had big receptions, and I wasn't afraid
    to shout ;
'Twas before the fine French notion of "acting
    charades" came out.
I'd my name on the six-feet posters, and big in the
    Drury bills ;
I think of it often now, lad, and my poor old bosom
    thrills.

I can see the stage and the footlights, and the house
    and the crowded pit ;
I can hear the shouts and the stamping that tell me
    I've made a hit ;
I can see the sea of faces flash white as I cross the
    scene.
Ah me! but those triumphs, Charley, they were
    few and too far between.

I was always weak and ailing, and I hadn't the best
  of luck;
I got the fame that I worked for, but somehow it
  never stuck.
There wasn't a run on Shakespeare, or the manage-
  ment broke down,
And I had to take to the country, and work from
  town to town.

So I couldn't have saved much money—not with a
  wife to keep
And three young children, Charley—that's one of
  them there asleep.
The wife she died one winter—she died of a broken
  heart;
She'd to play in a play called "Troubles," and hers
  was a killing part.
And I was left with the children to do the best I
  could,
But I got in the bills in London, and that winter
  God was good.
I made a success, and was lucky, the play ran half
  a year,
So I paid up my back debts bravely—and then I
  was taken queer.

One day I was on the hoardings, in letters quite two
    feet high,
And the next I was lying here, lad, and they thought
    that I should die ;
But I lingered and mended slowly, and here I am
    lying still—
With the last of my savings vanished, and a terrible
    doctor's bill.
Oh ! it's hard when the black ox bellows, and comes
    with his cruel tread
To scatter our earthly treasures, and crush our
    ambition dead ;
To know that the world we worked for has never a
    thought to spare,
But worships a brand-new hero who reigns in the
    footlights' glare.

Charley, I'm glad to see you, for there's something
    I want to say,
Now I know that the Lord has called me, and my
    life ebbs fast away.
It haunts me asleep and waking, and it fills me with
    nameless fear ;
What will become of my darlings when I am no
    longer here ?

An actor is soon forgotten—he reigns as a king
　　awhile :
He's fêted, and cheered, and honoured, and he basks
　　in the public's smile.
But the moment his work is over, and gone is the
　　power to please,
He has drained the cup of pleasure and come to
　　the bitter lees.

Then he whom the thousands greeted with a tempest
　　of hearty cheers,
Who passed as a conquering hero 'mid the homage
　　of crowded tiers,
May lie in his bitter anguish, and moan with the
　　ceaseless pain,
With never a word to soothe him, and he cries for
　　help in vain.
Oh, it's hard to be thus forgotten ! to know, as the
　　years roll by,
You are fading from all remembrance, you who
　　had climbed so high ;
It's hard, in the sad night watches, to think how you
　　once could play,
And to know that the curtain's fallen which hides
　　you, alas ! for aye.

O for the fire that nerved me when I trod the busy
    scene,
In the glory of plume and helmet and my armour's
    silver sheen !
O for the mad wild rapture as I fought the mimic
    fight,
And the house rose nightly at me and yelled with a
    fierce delight !
I am watched by the eager thousands, and their hot
    flushed faces turn—
As I cry in a voice of thunder that the traitor's
    threat I spurn ;
Then forth flies my white steel flashing, and I smite
    at the tyrant—so,
And he reels to the wings and staggers 'neath the
    weight of the ringing blow.

Hark at the people, Charley !—hark at the mighty
    roar !
It floats in my ears like music that shall come again
    no more.
Prop me a bit with the pillows—I'm faint, and my
    sight grows dim ;
The thought of the past unnerves me, and I tremble
    in every limb.

I've lain here a helpless cripple, so long in this dull
    back room,
That I've grown half a corpse already ; this is but
    a living tomb.
Oh, it's cruel to lie and ponder, as the twilight slowly
    falls,
On the scene that lies out yonder and the crowd in
    Drury's walls.

I can hear the soft sweet music, I can see the dear
    old baize,
And I look in the morning paper through the list of
    the promised plays.
Then my eyes are closed in fancy, and right through
    the walls I see,
And the lamps in the Strand are lighted, and the
    folks come two and three,
Till a big crowd slowly gathers and stretches across
    the street ;
Then the pit door opens sharply, and I hear the
    tramping feet ;
And the quiet pro's pass onward to the stage-door
    up the court—
Ah ! I feel like a dying schoolboy, who watches his
    comrades' sport.

I've done with the stage for ever, but I'll love it till
    I die.
. Charley, one word, old fellow, before we say good-
    bye.
It's time for you to be going ; let me look at your
    face once more ;
You'll be on the boards directly, and you'll hear the
    welcome roar.
I've a secret, lad, to tell you—I've kept it up till
    now—
But I know whose hand is laying the chills on my
    aching brow ;
I smother my pride to ask it ; but, Charley, when
    I am dead,
Don't let me think my children may know the want
    of bread.

My poor little hoard of savings has melted long
    ago—
'Twas a secret I meant, God willing, the world
    should never know.
I've schemed and I've planned and worried, and
    parted with all we had,
And kept the poor home together with the help of
    my eldest lad.

When I'm gone you may tell my story : how, keep-
    ing the wolf at bay,
In torture of soul and body, the poor old actor
    lay,
Forgotten by all his fellows.   But, let it go far and
    wide,
'Twas the thought of his starving children that con-
    quered the father's pride.

MISCELLANEOUS.

MISCELLANEOUS.

THE LIGHTS OF LONDON TOWN.*

THE way was long and weary,
　　But gallantly they strode,
A country lad and lassie,
　　Along the heavy road.
The night was dark and stormy,
　　But blithe of heart were they,
For shining in the distance
　　The Lights of London lay.
O gleaming lamps of London that gem the City's
　　crown,
What fortunes lie within you, O Lights of London
　　Town.

* Set to music by Louis Diehl, and published by Boosey and Co., 242,
Regent-street, W.

The years passed on and found them
  Within the mighty fold,
The years had brought them trouble,
  But brought them little gold.
Oft from their garret window,
  On long still summer nights,
They'd seek the far-off country
  Beyond the London lights.
O mocking lamps of London, what weary eyes
  look down,
And mourn the day they saw you, O Lights of
  London Town.

With faces worn and weary,
  That told of sorrow's load,
One day a man and woman
  Crept down a country road.
They sought their native village,
  Heart-broken from the fray ;
Yet shining still behind them,
  The Lights of London lay.
O cruel lamps of London, if tears your light could
  drown,
Your victims' eyes would weep them, O Lights of
  London Town.

SENSATIONAL SCIENCE.

———◆———

HE rage for knowledge grows apace,
　　A pace that quite terrific is;
To-day the whole of Britain's race
　　Devoutly scientific is.

No more in cloisters science roams,
　　No tyrant gives a knock to it;
It writes, we rush to buy its tomes;
　　It lectures, and we flock to it.

For science now our girls and boys
　　Their love for thee recant, O mime!
The clown is shunned for higher joys,
　　And Tyndall beats the pantomime.

The " Institution " lectures draw
　　The babes who once loved merriment;
And tiny tots can lisp the law
　　That governs each experiment.

Our laughing girls give up their play,
 All bitten by the mania
To hear what Huxley has to say
 On Patagonian crania.

Ethnology bids croquet stand,
 And cast aside lawn tennis is
For Evolution's doctrines and
 The charms of Biogenesis.

On Life and Death and Hell (O fie!)
 These famous men enlighten us:
They wing their flight so very high
 They positively frighten us.

On all our cherished creeds they fall,
 Without the least apology,
And hurl the bowl that scatters all
 The ninepins of theology.

We sit enthralled when Huxley shows,
 Or writes about, in articles,
The stream of life that ebbs and flows
 In protoplasmic particles.

And when the microscope reveals
  What lies in specks gelatinous,
The timid maiden almost squeals,
  "O dear, to think we've *that* in us!"

Then Darwin says that our papas—
  (Is't science this or lunacy?)—
Ran up the trees with our mammas
  In man's old world, Baboonacy.

Our girls, from views so wild as these,
  Half angry and half funky rise;
To say they come from chimpanzees
  Does make the darlings' monkey rise.

"Art-culture" leads a giddy throng,
  Who ape the strict æsthetical,
And think the "pretty" must be wrong,
  The "tidy" quite heretical.

The critic's jargon, quickly caught,
  Is lisped by girls at boarding-school!
And Art's at present largely taught
  According to the "hoarding-school."

Grim Ruskin frowns and hurls his darts,
   And lifts his voice to lecture all
On painting, sculpture, and the arts,
   And topics architectural.

In Ruskin's page all dip awhile,
   For quaint and clever Ruskin is;
As " pitching in " pervades his style,
   The world of readers thus kin is.

Like Tyndall, Huxley, Darwin, he
   Must now and then his quarrels have;
But all of them the great B.P.
   Encrowned with lavish laurels have.

Explain, O Truth, why men like these
   Are heroes educational!
Miss Truth replies, " Why, if you please,
   Because they're so sensational!"

THE BUTTERCUP'S EXPLANATION.

HAPPENED last week by the merest of chances
   To wander at noon near a sweet little spot,
When the May sun was casting its warmest of glances
   And making the baa-lambs believe it was hot.
It's true that the joke lasted only a moment,
   For just as a buttercup lifted its head
To see what its sudden sensation of glow meant,
   Young Phœbus grew frightened and hastily fled.

I fancied I noticed that buttercup's petals
   Assume an undoubted expression of scorn,
For even a buttercup's feelings it nettles
   To find that our springtide of sunshine is shorn.
In mood philosophic, the why and the wherefore
   Of all that attracts my attention I seek ;
Its mind on the state of the weather I therefore
   Invited that floweret freely to speak.

" You ask me," it answered, " my private conclusion
    Respecting these obstinate fits of the sun ;
Now I think, though it may be an empty delusion,
    That science the worst of the mischief has done.
You know there's a theory—Huxley's and Tyndall's—
    That the whole of mankind and the animate world
Take their life from the heat which his majesty kindles,
    And, losing it, all would to chaos be hurled ?

" I guess the sun's heard that his sway is despotic,
    The words of the savants have come to his ears,
No longer earth's lover with vigour quixotic,
    Now seldom among us his lordship appears.
Like the swell who presides at a charity dinner,
    He fancies his ' form ' is so awfully good ;
And feels with the pride of a privileged sinner
    He's much too important to come when he should."

LITTLE JIM.

UR little Jim
 Was such a limb
 His mother scarce could manage
  him.
His eyes were blue,
And looked you through,
And seemed to say,
" I'll have my way ! "
His age was six,
His saucy tricks
But made you smile,
Though all the while
You said, " You limb,
You wicked Jim,
  Be quiet, do ' "

Poor little Jim!
Our eyes are dim
When soft and low we speak of him.
No clatt'ring shoe
Goes running through
The silent room,
Now wrapped in gloom.
So still he lies,
With fast-shut eyes,
No need to say,
Alas! to-day,
" You little limb,
You baby Jim,
Be quiet, do!"

A COMMON OCCURRENCE.

I HAD a dream the other night—
   A vision I should rather say—
In which I climbed to fortune's height
   In quite a sudden sort of way.
When half asleep and half awake
   A flash of inspiration came,
And showed me something that would make
   A boundless wealth and lasting fame.

I think I hit upon a plan
   Of doing something long decreed
A feat impossible to man,
   Of which he stood in special need.
It might have been to make a gas
   At twopence per the thousand feet,
Or farthing dinners for the mass
   To take the place of butchers' meat.

I know that in my semi-dream
   I saw the thing as clear as noon,
With not a hitch in all the scheme,
   Which gave the world a priceless boon.
'Twas no inventor's fancy task,
   But simple as the A B C ;
Yet now I beat my brow and ask,
   What could that splendid notion be ?

For days and days I've taxed my brain
   To bring that blessed vision back,
But all my efforts are in vain,
   I can't get Fancy on the track.
A chance of fortune, so they say,
   Comes once to all men here below,
Mine caught me napping, passed away,
   And what it was I ne'er shall know.

THE POLICEMAN'S TALE.

AFTER CHAUCER—500 YEARS.

———•———

CONSTABEL one nighte that it didde
  rayne
Both cattes and dogges, and pytchforkes
  too, was fayne
Hymsel within a taverne to betake,
His flesch to drie, and eke hys thyrste to slake.
And there ful many a pleasaunt carle he founde
In barr-parloure a grogge-bowle seaten rounde,
Y-like hymsel who'd soughten herbergage
Ontil ye storme its furie sholde assuage.
Ye canne went rounde and pypes of claye were litte,
And everichone y-didde what seemed hym fytte,
Til whan no wight colde hearen hymsel speke.
Up gat ye Hoste, a burgess bigge in cheke,
And this he sayde unto them plat and playne:
" An' here ye wolden bide ontil ye rayne

I

Hath stayed itsel, in sooth, then baren ye
With les dispute and more tranquillitie.
To passe ye time I trowe it wolde be wel,
An everichone in tourne a tayle sholde tel,
And thilkë wight who in hys taske do fayle
Shal paye his comperes rounde in moisty ayle."
Then sotte he doune; the guestës cried " Y-wis,"
And castë lottes who firste sholde doen this.
Ye Constabel ye longest wispë drewe,
And thus beganne withouten more ado.

YE CONSTABEL HIS TAYLE.

Whilom whan newë to ye force I came
And modest was nor uppe to everich game,
Nor wot for naught that I might laye a hande
On any common carle in Englelande.
It fell one nighte that it was drear and wette
(My beate was in ye pleasaunt Haimaurkette),
A manne I spied y-fallen on ye grounde,
And straighte didde kikke hym for to bring hym
      rounde;
And whan maugré my kikkes no signe he mayd,
Hym through ye streete I by hys heeles conveyed,
And to the Stacioun did hym dragge, the where
Ye Sergeaunt straight y-clapt hym in a chayre;

But as he wolde ne speke, ne ope hys eyes,
Though with our beltës we hym did chasteyse,
Eftsoons, we felled him ; he of drinke did smelle,
So hym we casten in ye tosspottes celle.

Now whan that morne was come much was I payned
To finde this caitiffe on hys bakke remayned.
In vaine by bearde I swinked hym to and fro ;
He wolde ne smyle, ne answour " aye " ne " noe,"
But stille he laye with eyen fast y-shet,
And on hys legges I colde him no way get.
I hayled a cabbe and stecked hym on ye scate,
Than with hym drove to Courte of Bowës-streete ;
Agen ye dokke I stecked hym bolte uprite,
An I to ye Judge hys deedës did recyte.
How that I founde ye gaillard on ye grounde,
And that sin' then hys tongue he hed not founde.
" Thy name ? " freined Judge, and set on hym hys
    eye.
And still ye carle vouchsafëd no replye.
" He sickerley shammes ille," ye Judge did shoute ;
" Let leeche be highte, we'll see this mattere outte."
Ye leeche he came, and criëd with amayze ·
" Marry ! thys carle's been deadë all two dayes."

Hyr ceased ye Constabel and looked aboute,
Espëring to have hearde a merrie shoute ;

But everich fayce was blakke, and one manne rose
And shoke hys fiste beneath ye peeler's nose,
And cryed that it was shame in Christen lande
Such fools should holde mennes livës in their hande.
"Graunt-mercy for yr tayle, gode Sir," quod he,
"It showth what doltes are in auctoritie."
And than he tolde how he hymsel hadde sene
A manne nigh deade tway constabels betwene,
Who shoke hym wel and called hym dronken loon,
And kikkëd hym with iron-tippëd shoon.
By this ye rayne had ceased, which, whan they knew,
Ye guestës rose and went outte two by two.
Ye Constabel was called to stoppe a fraye,
So drank his ayle and wente another waye.

AN ASPIRATION.

WOULD I might have had the luck
   To live some million years ago,
   Ere man emerging from the ruck
Contrived so many things to know;
Ere sense of sin could mar his rest,
   And laws had not invented crimes.
No qualms of conscience life opprest
   Say those who write of early times.

The world was once a baking ball
   Of dirt and other nasty things,
And then there were no men at all,
   So clever Mr. Tyndall sings.
I'll follow back creation's scale,
   And wish I had existed then,
A shapeless something with a tail,
   A shallow mudbank for my den.

These monsters lived a thousand years
  In one delightful semi-doze,
Untouched by either hopes or fears
  Amid formation's thousand throes.
They wallowed on in lazy mood
  With indolent, half-open eye,
And jaws agape to catch the food
  The sluggish stream brought floating by.

The cake got harder, and the earth
  With each new layer fitter grew
To give a noble creature birth
  Till men at last its forest knew.
They tilled the long untortured soil,
  And warred against the prowling beasts,
Till life became one long turmoil
  Of work and sport and bloody feasts.

As onward still the ages rolled
  Came Culture with its blasting breath,
To bid the ills of life unfold
  And give new pangs and fears to death.
With weakened muscles, quickened nerves,
  With aching limbs and heated brain,
Our race to-day from nature swerves,
  And life becomes an overstrain.

And when the strife was at its height,
  My span of wild unrest began,
Fate pounced upon this luckless wight
  And set him here a modern man.
A worried, bustled, nervous thing,
  A victim of the age of steam ;
With tearful eyes and hands that wring,
  Of pre-historic times I dream.

Kind Fortune come, my woes assuage,
  Bend down and mark a modern's moan,
And bear me through the golden age,
  Through times of Iron, Bronze, and Stone !
Back, back before the men with tails,
  A million years before the Flood,
To where the search of science fails,
  And leave me happy in the mud.

IN THE HALL.

COME in New Year and wipe your feet,
　　And shake the snow that's clinging,
I'm glad the little man to meet
　For whom the bells are ringing.
You bow your head, and smirk and smile,
　　And squeeze my hand the tighter;
Your honest eyes look free from guile—
　　You could not be politer.

I know the words your lips would form,
　　I've heard the greeting often—
" I come as sunshine after storm,
　　Your recent blows to soften."
Bah ! foolish boy, you'll learn to strike,
　　Or e'er your boyhood mellows;
The years, alas ! are all alike—
　　A band of wicked fellows.

UNDERTONES.

BY A LUNATIC LAUREATE.

———◆———

THERE'S a feeling that comes with the daze of joy
    And goes with the knights of grief—
That stands on the top of a baby buoy,
    And floats with an anchor chief.
It rides on the back of a noted Bill,
    And fights where your collars fray;
It whispers in accents loud and shrill—
    To-morrow succeeds to-day.

We con the lessons of life betimes
    In the leaves of an open glade;
The frost on the window writes its rimes,
    We live and we learn be trayed.
The coals we heat and the apes we were
    Are gone where the Russians sleigh.
The moral is blown on the well-known air—
    To-morrow succeeds to-day.

In the bustle and jam of the daily strife,
   What matters if men preserve
The bosom of hope from the butcher's knife,
   And its train from the pointsman curve?
Remember the fate of the ready maid
   Who went where the preachers prey
Take matter for thought from a new decayed—
   To-morrow succeeds to-day.

MY ARCTIC TOUR.

I HAVE not the least ambition—this is explanation merely—
 For a winter in the regions that are handy to the Pole,
Yet I imitate the travels of the heroes that have nearly,
 'Mid such horrible adventures, won the tantalising goal.

I have followed Captain Parry to the islands that he christened,
 Where his vessel lay imprisoned all the weary winter through ;
I have been with Ross and Beechey where the frozen ocean glistened,
 Where no animal would linger and no vegetation grew.

I have watched the starving sailors of the Erebus
  and Terror,
And my well-pomatumed tresses have uplifted at
  the roots
When I saw the gallant fellows fall, alas! into the
  error,
That a stay for empty stomachs was a rotten pair
  of boots.

I have sailed with Kane, M'Clintock, Osborne,
  Kennedy, and others,
And I've trodden the Polaris with the doughty
  Captain Hall,
I have rivalled all the actions of the band of Polar
  brothers,
I have been with Nares to Disco,—but in fancy—
  that is all.

When the twilight shadows deepen and my daily
  work is over,
Home I hasten to the suburbs where my habitation
  lies ;
There I don the proper garment for a Pole-
  exploring rover,
I have learned its cut and texture in the " Travels "
  that I prize.

Next, I hoist the British ensign on the sofa (that's
    my vessel),
Strew the floor with bits of paper as a substitute
    . for snow,
Sail for Disco (that's the table), where I ask if
    sister Bess 'll,
For a small consideration, be my faithful
    Eskimo.

When by dint of much exertion with the poker and
    the shovel,
We have brought our gallant vessel right across the
    parlour floor,
We have reached our Winter quarters, neither
    money, strength, nor love 'll
Cleave a passage through the iceberg represented
    by the door.

Hence we sledge upon the teatray o'er the ice-
    encumbered ocean,
But our latitude's uncertain and our longitude is
    vague,
And we rub each other's noses just to keep alive
    the notion
That we suffer from the nippings which the Arctic
    heroes plague.

In some four-and-twenty journeys, we've discovered
    all the stations
Where adventurers before us passed so many
    weary days,
And in turn we gave the honour of our winter
    occupations—
Behring Strait and Melville Island, Great Fish
    River and the Bays.

As for climate—well, it needed very little to
    instil a
Perfect sense of frigid horrors, since it's easy on
    the whole
For a man who spends the winter *in a new
suburban villa,* .
To imagine that he's braving all the rigours of the
    Pole.

A CHANGE FOR THE BETTER.

OMEWHERE or other in History's page
I've read that when poets were all the rage,—
    (Oh, History, thou detractor!)—
They'd only to scribble a puff in verse,
To make them free of the house and purse
    Of a titled benefactor.

What halcyon days they must have been,
When lords were ready to step between
    The bard and slow starvation ;
When a poet had only to praise a peer,
To earn a couple of "thou" a year
    And a Government situation.

The bard may struggle and fight to-day
And charm the town with his tuneful lay
    No hand is stretched to aid him ;
He sells his song to the trading crew,
Who hand him a paltry pound or two
    And think they've overpaid him.

Yet now, my brothers, our pens are free,
We flatter no ninny of high degree,
    Because his favours pay so.
No titled patron's help we crave,
And if we think that a nob's a knave,
    We've every right to say so.

Let Fortune's wheel bring ceaseless blanks,
Let Destiny play us her wildest pranks,
    And Misery come to try us ;
We're better by far than the bards of old—
By many a man we may be sold,
    But nobody's wealth can buy us.

THE DRINKER'S DIRGE

HERE'S death in the teapot, there's
    death in the jug ;
  Try a drain of cold water, death lurks in
    the mug.
No drink unfermented from danger is free,
There are death and disease in Milk, Water, and Tea.

From the lead that in "waters" is lurking I shrink—
Oh, tell me, good doctors, what, what can I drink ?
From the worship of Bacchus a convert I'd be,
Yet you bid me beware of Milk, Water, and Tea.

How a total abstainer's to live isn't clear,
For his conscience forbids him Wine, Spirits, and Beer :
And Science commands as from death he should flee
From those poisonous liquids, Milk, Water, and Tea.

In trying from all things our lips to debar
Hasn't Science just galloped his hobby too far ?
Let the nervous go thirsting, they sha'n't frighten me
With this nonsense concerning Milk, Water, and Tea.

THE ALDERMAN'S RETROSPECT.

I N vain the board with silver groans
　　And fumes of turtle rise,
　　He only heaves a sigh and moans
　As each new dish he tries;
For Indigestion mounts her seat
　And Appetite departs:
Ah! happy days when he could eat
　A shilling's-worth of tarts.

Go hide the capon from his sight,
　Remove that *ris de veau*,
For every taste he takes to-night
　Increases gastric woe.
Now back o'er many a distant day
　His wand'ring fancies run;
A lanky lad he puts away
　Six penn'orth underdone.

Lo! o'er his thin-stemmed goblet's brim
　The sparkling nectar creams.
Its lips are left unkissed by him—
　He bows his head and dreams.
Once more at night, a hungry boy,
　He leaves his master's shop,
And sups upon a saveloy
　Washed down with ginger pop.

A friendly nudge prevents the snore
　That rises to his nose ;
He picks his napkin from the floor,
　And shifts his gouty toes.
Yet still his thoughts will backward flee,
　And, racked by many a pain,
He'd give his hard-won wealth to be
　That hungry boy again.

THE JOKE.

I HAD a joke—a little joke,
   I told it humbly far and near,
No laugh the solemn stillness broke,
   But people gazed with eyes severe,
And seem'd to think I should be hit
For thinking such a thing was wit.

I asked some critics to my room,
   And gave it over Moët's best.
There fell on all a sudden gloom,
   And low I hid my fallen crest.
" Don't make such sorry jokes," they said,
" But cut another quart instead."

I took my joke and wrapped it up,
   And spun it out a yard or two,
Then sought a well-known place to sup,
   Where lots of clever men I knew.
Then sitting down I cried forthwith,
" Who knows this joke of Sydney Smith?"

They clustered round me while I told
   My little joke as Sydney's child;
With frantic mirth about they rolled
   And e'en the sleepy waiters smiled.
What, reader, could the reason be?
They laughed at him and sneered at me!

I fancy, if you think it out,
   You'll find the men who hear a jest
Are often harassed by a doubt
   If mirth or scorn would look the best.
By few the jokes are understood,
But Sydney Smith's!—they *must* be good

HARMONIOUS NUMBERS.

A SOUVENIR.

JUST pass your pouch this way, old fellow,
   We've only time for twenty whiffs,
For through the sunlight mild and mellow
   I see the chalk of Dover cliffs.
Ere daylight be with darkness blended
   Our joyous journey will be done,
A pleasant page of life's book ended
   For Fifty-seven and Sixty-one.

But yester eve and we were sipping
   A *mazagrin* beneath the trees,
Parisian loungers past us tripping,
   And all was there the eye to please.
Till late we sat, 'twas past eleven
   When home we went with jest and pun,
And sought our rooms—I Fifty-seven,
   And you, old fellow, Sixty-one.

But yesterday and we were driving
   In Boulogne's wood so fresh and green,
Where light and shade were gently striving
   Which best could paint the sylvan scene.
From Notre Dame, 'twixt earth and heaven,
   We gazed on Paris bathed in sun,
Then arm-in-arm with Fifty-seven
   To dine went *ami* Sixty-one.

My pipe's gone out!　Hulloa, here's Dover!
   Pick up your traps, old boy, we're in!
Our holiday, alas! is over;
   Now hey! for London's dirt and din.
Some grief all earthly joys must leaven,
   We part to-night, our course is run.
You won't forget old Fifty-seven—
   Good-bye.　God bless you, Sixty-one!

MY SUMMER RETREAT.

'M off away from London, please, to build
a little place
Where I can have some air to breathe and
lots of open space;
I want to find a mountain top that isn't over bleak,
Without a hilly road to it, because my legs are weak.

I do not want a neighbourhood beset with country
clowns,
But just a neighbour here and there who knows the
way of towns.
They must not come and call on me, for callers are
a bore,
But I shall go and visit them say twice a week or
more.

I want the country round about to be the sort of
thing
Of which the chaps who write for books perpetually
sing—
Renowned throughout the British Isles as just the
place to see;
But all the country round about I want reserved to
me.

I want the strict simplicity of rural life to reign
O'er wooded height and shady dell and daisy-dotted
plain;
But there must be a station close and frequent trains
must start
To run me at a modest fare to almost every part.

No echo of the city life must find its way to mar,
I want no village public-house with yokels at the bar;
But just a dainty restaurant where haply I may
dine,
And find a perfect French cuisine and get the best
of wine.

REGRET.

DO not mourn, sweet wife of mine,
Because those ruby lips of thine—
      That marble brow—
Were kissed by one who might have been,
Had I not chanced to step between,
      Thy husband now.

I do not grieve because thy heart,
Ere Cupid touched it with *my* dart,
      For him would beat:
Nor that the hand which owns my ring
Once wore his gift, a " Mizpah " thing.
      It was but meet.

I sigh not that his arms were placed
Some score of times around your waist,
      So sweet and slim.
Ah no, my love! the woe you see
Is mine because you wedded me
      Instead of him.

A RONDEL.

CHASING dead leaves along the thick
    strewn way,
    Madly we hurry for the rough wind's prey.
  Caught by the colours which false Fancy weaves,
Our godlike youth in aimless sports we slay.
    Fair is the outset; 'tis the goal that grieves,
        Chasing dead leaves.

Chasing dead leaves! Oh, wife with care-dulled eyes,
Far back our start upon the journey lies.
  Where is Hope's harvest, all the golden sheaves?
Where of linked lives is now the promised prize?
    Spring noons are past, we come to Autumn eves,
        Chasing dead leaves.

Chasing dead leaves! shall Fame not turn to one
Gleaming so brightly in the morning sun?
  Who dons a verdure that fond youth deceives
And hides the canker till the race is run:
    Then mocks the clutch of him whose bosom heaves,
        Chasing dead leaves.

A TRUE STORY.

T happened that an Eastern King,
  Whose name and land I need not
    mention,
Came over here to try and bring
  His troubles to our folks' attention.
Our gracious sovereign heard his tale,
  Our leading statesmen all received him,
And though his story turned them pale,
  They heard it through and quite believed him.

He told them how his subjects were
  Composed of races vile and vicious;
He laid their awful secrets bare,
  And proved the moment most propitious
For us to send our teachers out
  (With such a wish what State could quarrel?)
To put their wicked ways to rout
  And inculcate the strictly moral.

Now while the chosen men prepare
  To start upon their noble mission,
The monarch has a month to spare
  In which to study our position.
He learns our language, sees our sights.
  And cuts the usual tourist capers,
Sees London life in all its lights,
  And takes to read the daily papers.

Or rather—let me be correct—
  He only read a single journal.
Its leaders caused him to reflect ;
  The "cases" gave him pangs internal
He read of kickings, bitings, blows,
  Of murders, fights, and frauds, and arsons ;
Of swindlers charged in lengthy rows,
  Including doctors, nobs, and parsons.

He read the sheet with horrors fraught,
  His eyes were fixed in wildest terror,
His Christian friends at once he sought
  And begged their pardon for his error.
"I see," he said, "'twere wrong to take
  Your teachers from their present labours,
However much their hearts may ache
  For wickedness among their neighbours.

" My subjects are, I grieve to state,
    By much removed from virtue's standard.
It has distressed me, too, of late
    To find they all to crime have pandered.
But having seen your stock of vice,
    Of sin, and shame, and degradation,
I feel my folks are clean and nice;
    Compared with you—a spotless nation."

THE HUMAN AUCTION.

HO! here are lives by the score to sell.
  Up to the platform, gents, and bid;
Make me an offer, they'll pay you well—
All of 'em ripe for the coffin lid.
Here is a woman pinched and pale,
  Plying her needle for daily bread;
Give me a shirt for her—more on sale,
  Dying! gentlemen—dying!—dead!

A family, six in number, here,
  Fresh from a cellar in Somers' Town;
Mother her sixth confinement near,
  Father and brats with fever down.
'Twas Pestilence spoke then, was it not?
  "An open sewer," I think he said;
Well, his offer shall buy the lot,
  Dying! gentlemen—dying!—dead!

Now, good customers, here's a chance:
   A thousand men in the prime of life,
Wielders of musket, sword, and lance,
   Armed and drilled for the deadly strife.
General Warfare lifts his hand—
   " A bullet for each," cries the gent in red.
No offer but his,—fast flows the sand,
   Dying! gentlemen—dying!—dead !

A body of toilers worn and weak,
   Clerks and curates and writing men—
Look at the flush on each sunken cheek,
   Mark the fingers that grasp the pen !
Come, good gentlemen, can't we deal?
   Has Drudgery's eye for bargains fled ?
He offers, at last, the price of a meal—
   Dying! gentlemen—dying!—dead !

A LEGEND.

BY A LUNATIC LAUREATE.

———◆———

THEY came to me, a merry troop of aged
    men and dames,
And bade me brighten up a bit and watch
    their little games.
I had my big umbrella up and stood beneath a tree,
And so I said, "It's much too wet to lark about and
    spree."
The skies above were black as ink, the rain was
    pouring down,
And boats would be the only means to reach the
    distant town.
'Twas in the height of summer time—in fact, an
    August day,
Yet I was damp and had no heart to slush about and
    play.

L

So, when they saw that I was sad, those aged
    people went
And brought me out a macintosh, goloshes, and a
    tent,
And sat them down on stools and things and told
    me little tales
Of how in August years ago there were no awful
    gales;
Of how the summer days were warm and folks could
    play about,
And never dread the hurricane, the storm, and
    waterspout ;
How people romped in new-mown hay and had no
    end of fun,
And no one's eyes expressed surprise to see a
    noonday sun.

And when they saw the wonderment expressed upon
    my face,
They told me how the country once was quite a
    lovely place ;
Where one could sit upon the grass and gather
    wholesome fruits,
And walk about the verdant fields in patent leather
    boots.

How people then who went away a fortnight out of
    town
Came back with freckles on the nose and faces
    ruddy brown,
And how the summer sun shone out through all the
    summer time,
And rain and cold were looked upon as strangers to
    the clime.

I stood it for a little while, and then I rose and
    said :
" I wonder if the Devil put this nonsense in your
    head ?
I know I am a lunatic, but, hang it all, I say,
You story-telling aged folks, pack up and go away !
In summer we expect the gale, the tempest and the
    storm,
And only fools would dare to say it once was fine
    and warm.
Be off before yon summer cloud that blackens all
    the skies
In indignation drenches you for telling me such
    lies ! "

THE ENGLISHMAN.

ROM infancy, which crows and crawls,
    To years mature, which sigh and run,
  He lives where rain eternal falls
  And seldom comes a gleam of sun.
Above his head are blackened clouds,
  Below a slush that never dries,
While chill and drenching moisture shrouds
  The dismal land of leaden skies.

What wonder if his features bear
  The reflex of his sunless clime:
A settled look of dull despair
  Set deeply by the hand of Time!
What wonder if the ceaseless drip
  Of raindrops from the soaking eaves
Takes hold of him with rolling grip,
  And just a mildewed mortal leaves!

He cannot dance or sing or laugh
    Like children of the brighter South;
To keep his soul warm he must quaff
    A liquid fire that stings the mouth,
That thaws the heart and melts the brain,
    That sets a Devil in his eyes,—
So Demon Drink and Demon Rain
    Rule all the land of leaden skies.

THE HAUSFRAUENVEREIN.

ITHIN that most malod'rous city,
 Whence Papal bishops have to flee !
 Where folks are rather wise than witty,
And yet for ever on the Spree,—
The housewives lately have decided
 In one strong body to combine,
To deal with questions many-sided,
 And form a Hausfrauenverein.

When tradesmen give short weight and measure,
 When doctors' charges get too high,
When fashion interferes with pleasure
 And single men from wedlock fly—
These fair ones quickly hold a sitting,
 And straight determine on the line
Of warfare which is most befitting
 The Berlin Hausfrauenverein.

They fix the price of beef and mutton,
   They frame the laws of ball and rout,
Discuss the claims of hook or button,
   And trot their whims and crotchets out.
How much by ladies may be swallowed
   Of Wiener Bier, or Rhenish wine,
The rule is made, and strictly followed
   By all the Hausfrauenverein.

The best attention by them paid is
   To all the laws their lords propose
Which bear at all upon the ladies;
   They aid their friends and fight their foes.
Now here's a plan, dear Woman's Righters,—
   Why not like Berlin dames combine?
Leave Westminster to fiercer fighters,
   And form a Hausfrauenverein.

LITTLE WORRIES.

THOUGH many ills may hamper life
   When Fortune turns capricious,
   The great but nerve us for the strife,
  The small ones make us vicious.
Fierce griefs are soon outstripped by one
  Who through existence scurries;
It's harder far a race to run
  With nimble "little worries."

A button bids your shirt good-bye
  When late for dinner dressing,
You have a kite you cannot fly,
  And creditors are pressing.
You run to catch—and lose—a train
  (That fatalest of hurries),
Your newest hat encounters rain—
  Life's full of "little worries."

From day to day some silly things
    Upset you altogether ;
There's nought so soon convulsion brings
    As tickling with a feather.
'Gainst minor evils let him pray
    Who fortune's favour curries,—
For one that big misfortunes slay
    Ten die of "little worries."

YE BARDES DESYRE.

N I of formes to tak my choyce
  Were at this momente free, .
 I'd be ye birde whose tuneful voyce
  I heere on yonder tree.
He onlye singes whan he's inclynde;
  Hys constitucion's sounde;
Ande he has ne ye rente to fynde
  Whan Quartere Daye commes rounde.

From twigge to twigge he hoppes aboute,
  No woes his harte oppress,
And whan at morne he turneth oute
  He has not gotte to dress.
'Tis true hys songe he has to synge
  Withoute a syngers fee,
But that's about ye onlye thynge
  In which oure lottes agree.

ON A RECENT LITERARY FEED.

 HAT, eat a newspaper!" quoth Tim.
   " Pray did the meal agree with him ;
   Or did he indigestion get,
The man who thus a journal ate ?
I read the papers every day,
And ne'er can swallow *half* they say."

" From such a feast," Tim's friend replies,
" How could dyspeptic pains arise ?
The Press would scarce eschew its rule
To spite the chest of such a fool.
And papers, so the cynics sing,
Lie easily on anything."

A DOUBLE EVE-ENT.

 HEARD a matron on a Boat-race day
Applaud the pluck our British youth
   display—
And cry, with pride upon her beaming face,
She thought 'twas that which always won a race.
" Ah, madam," said I, "such ideas eschew,"
For Eden's river rises to my view :
There tempted, Eve, alas ! turns lady thief,
And by her *pluck* she brings *our race* to grief.

PRINTED AT 19 AND 20, WINE OFFICE-COURT, FLEET-STREET, E.C.